SAMBA SENSATION

Chloe Melody

Hodder
Children's
Books

A division of Hachette Children's Books

★ *Meet the Professional Dancers from* ★

Artem Chigvintsev

★ **Which three words best describe the samba to you?**

Carnival, party, fun.

★ **How old were you when you discovered you loved to dance?**

I was twelve. My mum loved dancing – just for fun, but her love of it encouraged me to give it a try and I'm glad I did!

★ **Did you go to a special dance academy like Bella?**

No, I learnt at home with my mum, but pretty soon I started taking lessons, although not at a proper dance academy.

★ **How old were you when you won your first dance competition?**

I was thirteen. Having taken dancing lessons and been encouraged by my mum to follow my heart and become a dancer it was a wonderful experience after only a year of dancing to compete with other boys and to be the winner!

★ **What is your favourite dance and why?**

Paso doble because it's dramatic, very physical but also is a feel good dance.

Turn the page to find out how Bella learns to dance the samba …

"Well, here we are," Bella's dad said
as they walked into the dorm room.
"The Strictly Dance Academy." He
grinned down at Bella. "Can you
believe it?"

"No." Bella let out a breath she hadn't
even realised she'd been holding.

Even though the auditions for
Strictly Come Dancing's Strictly Dance
Academy had finished a week ago,

Bella was still in shock. Had she really got into the academy? It hardly seemed possible when she thought of that long line of girls she'd been competing against. But somehow she'd made it, just by doing what her dad had told her – *dance like nobody's watching* – and it had worked!

Bella shivered with excitement as she tried to take in the room where she'd be sleeping. There was a bed under each of the three tall windows lining the long room and a fourth against one of the walls at the side. Each bed had a small wooden chest of drawers next to it and there was a large cupboard to hang clothes in by the door. The room was painted a pale yellow and the wooden floors had been polished until they glowed. *Perfect for practising routines on!* Bella thought. She wondered which of the ten Strictly Academy girls she'd be sharing with – she couldn't help hoping that Sofia and Natalie would be with her. They had really helped her get through the auditions, especially when she hadn't thought she'd make it. She'd never had any professional training after all, just dancing in a club at school, and some of the girls at the auditions had been dancing since they were really young. Bella might be in the academy, but she knew it would be seriously hard work to keep up with everyone else. She was going to need all the support she could get!

Bella sank down on the bed in front
of the middle window. After all the
dreaming, and all the ups and downs,
this was it. She was *really* here!

"Is that the bed you want then, love?"
Her dad picked up her bright red
suitcase,
ready to
lift it on to
the chest of
drawers.

"I suppose so – if the other girls won't mind."

Her dad laughed. "I should think their heads will be too full of dancing to mind which bed they sleep in."

Just then, Sofia walked in carrying her suitcase. Her dark hair was tied in a ponytail and she was wearing a green stripy T-shirt dress which looked lovely against her olive skin. Just behind her was a tall woman with black hair swept up into a neat glossy bun. She moved so gracefully across the floor that she almost seemed to float herself. Bella remembered Sofia had said that her mum had been a professional dancer in Italy.

She's so glamorous! Bella thought.

She felt a bit self-conscious as Sofia's mum swept into the room and gazed down at Bella. "Da*rrr*ling! Is this the friend you have been speaking about?"

"Hey, Bella!" Sofia grinned at her. "Yes, Mum, this is her."

"It is ve*rrr*y

wonderful to meet you!" Sofia's mum came closer and grabbed Bella's hands as she stood up from the bed. "My Sofia tells me you dance like an angel!" She pulled away one hand to kiss her fingertips and Bella had to tuck away a smile. Sofia's mum was *exactly* as Sofia had described her at the auditions – a real "*prrrima* ballerina"!

"It is ve*rrry* nice to meet you too," Sofia's mum told Bella's dad.

"I'm so glad we're in the same dorm," Sofia told Bella.

"So am I!"

"Hey, I hope you've saved a bed for me!" an American accent drawled. Bella turned to see Natalie grinning at her from the door. She was wearing jeans and a yellow long-sleeved T-shirt that had "Strictly Fabulous" printed on it.

"Of course we have," Bella laughed. "What about this one?" She pointed to the bed under the third window.

"Cool – the three of us in a row," Natalie said. "I just hope you don't snore!" She swung her case up on to the chest of drawers and then flopped on to the bed. "We had to get up really early to get ready, I'm exhausted already!"

"Not as exhausted as you'll be after we've started dance classes," Sofia told her. She prodded Natalie in her side. "You'd better get yourself unpacked."

Natalie groaned. "I guess so." She heaved herself up. "Where's my mom got to? She was right behind me."

Natalie's mum came in a second later carrying two long cardboard tubes. She couldn't have been more different from Sofia's mum, Bella thought. While Sofia's mum floated when she walked, Natalie's mum bounced along in her jeans and trainers. She had the same wide smile as Natalie. Bella immediately liked her. "Hey honey," she said to Natalie in a thick American accent. "I just went back to get these from the car – thought you might like to cheer up your room a little."

"My posters! Thanks, Mom!" Natalie took the tubes and pulled out three enormous posters of the Strictly Come Dancing professional dancers.

"What great posters!" Bella said.

"I'll help you put them up."

"Thanks!"

Bella noticed that Sofia had placed some postcards of prima ballerinas on her chest of drawers and was glad that she'd remembered to bring a photo of her mum and dad to put by her bed. They might not be famous dancers but it was down to them that she was here at all!

"We have to *share?*"

Bella's heart sank as she recognised the voice. She looked over to see Veronica standing in the doorway with a disgusted look on her face. Veronica's long blonde hair spilled out over the

shoulders of a tailored pink wool jacket which matched her pencil-thin trousers in a slightly darker shade of pink. Her dad appeared behind her with a mobile phone, held close to his ear.

"Yup," Natalie told her cheerfully. "That's your bed over there." She pointed at the bed against the wall.

"But—" Veronica was clearly about to complain about having the only bed without a window when her dad nudged her forward.

"Come on, sweetheart, Daddy's on an important call."

Veronica swept over to the bed by the wall while her dad barked into his phone. *"No*, it's *not* OK to push the deadline to tomorrow!" He tapped his smartphone to end the call and sighed heavily. "Have you got everything you need, beautiful?"

Veronica shook her head and pointed to the wardrobe. "I won't even have enough room to hang up my stuff if we've got to use the same cupboard!"

Natalie rolled her eyes at Bella. Bella found it difficult to suppress a giggle – Veronica was definitely a bit of a diva!

The parents began to say goodbye, kissing and hugging the four girls. Bella's dad squeezed her shoulder and whispered in her ear. "I'm really proud of you, you know."

"Thanks, Dad," she whispered back.

As soon as the girls were on their own, Veronica stalked over to Bella.

"I see you managed to get yourself the best bed," she said.

"Bella was here first, Veronica," Sofia told her.

"She shouldn't be here at all," Veronica snapped. "This place is for professionals, and she's just an amateur. Though they'll figure *that* out quickly enough."

Natalie stepped forward. "Look, Veronica, we're all roommates, so we need to get along. Understood?"

"Fine," Veronica said coldly. Then she turned on her heel and breezed out the door.

Bella felt her eyes sting with tears. Was Veronica right? Would she be kicked out once they realised that she was just a beginner?

Natalie shook her head. "My mom

would say she has an ego the size of an elephant."

"Yeah, she might be a good dancer but her personality could seriously do with a rehearsal!" Sofia glared after Veronica.

Bella gave them a watery smile. "Thanks, you two."

Natalie marched back up to Bella. "And you remember that you're here because you're a *great* dancer – OK?"

Bella laughed. Veronica might be horrible but her two new friends were more than making up for her. "OK!"

Just then a face appeared in the doorway. "Hi, girls!" An older girl of about fifteen came into the room. She was tall with long straight blonde hair

and large green eyes and
was wearing a leotard and
leggings with a short
wrap skirt in a beautiful
blue silky material.
Bella could see that
she was a dancer
from the way she
moved. Would Bella
ever look as confident
and professional as
she did?

The girl smiled at
them. "I'm Emma,
your dorm monitor.
I'll be looking after
you while you're here
and making sure you

get to where you need to be. And you already need to be somewhere!"

"We do?" Bella felt a ripple of excitement travel up her spine.

Emma nodded. "You have an audition in the academy ballroom in half an hour – they'll tell you all about it when you get there." She looked around. "Aren't there supposed to be four of you?"

Natalie nodded. "Veronica went somewhere – she didn't say where she was going."

"No problem, I'll find her. In the meantime, get your dancing clothes on and I'll be back in ten minutes to take you to the ballroom." She grinned. "And hey – good luck!"

After she'd left the girls looked at each other.

"Wow!" Natalie said, her brown eyes shining.

"I guess it's really starting," Sofia said.

Bella nodded, her heart thumping. The dream was definitely under way now!

2

Ten minutes later, the ten Strictly
Dance Academy girls in their dance
clothes were following as Emma led
the way. Bella wiggled her toes in her
brand new jazz shoes. They'd been a
congratulations present from her dad
when she got into the academy. She
kept sneaking peeks at her feet as she
walked – in her leotard, leggings and
wrap skirt, at last she was dressed like

a real dancer!

Emma explained that they had to report to the academy's reception area, and then they would go to the ballroom. Bella walked alongside Natalie and Sofia, enjoying the curious glances the group of girls were receiving from the people passing in the corridors. They must look really important!

They stopped in the same lobby Bella and her dad had come to for the auditions. Bella remembered how nervous she had been when she had seen the swarm of girls waiting to try out for a place in the academy. She felt another smile breaking through as she saw the wall of photos of the Strictly Come Dancing couples she'd noticed the first time she was here.

"It's so cool, isn't it?" Natalie said.

"Totally cool!" Bella said.

Emma gathered the group together. "OK, girls, you'll be getting a proper induction later on today but right now Ben Goodwin wants to see you for a special announcement about an audition."

Bella still couldn't believe they had an audition – they'd only just started!

There was no time to talk or ask questions. Emma handed out shiny passes on thin silver chains to hang around their necks which they would need to wear everywhere they went in the academy. Lots of television stars used the academy to rehearse in – including the Strictly Come Dancing celebrities – so they needed to have a pass like everyone else. Each pass had their photo on and were printed with the words *Strictly Dance Academy Dancer*. Bella gazed at the pass, her heart racing. *Dancer*. Seeing it in writing silenced her nerves for a moment. It reminded her of why she was here – because she really, really loved to dance . . .

"Let's get going!" Emma called out. "You don't want to be late for Ben Goodwin – you know what he's like about keeping time!"

The girls laughed and followed Emma

as she swept past the
reception desk, holding up
her pass. The girls copied
her as they walked
behind, the woman
at the reception desk
smiling and waving at
them. *It's like being a real celebrity!*
Bella thought.

The next moment Natalie nudged
her in the ribs. "Do you see him?" she
hissed.

"Who?" Bella peered in the direction
Natalie was angling her head and
gasped. It was Peter Evans, the host of
the BBC breakfast show!

"My dad always has him on," Sofia
whispered next to them. "He says he's

the best presenter on telly."

As they turned another corner, this time it was Bella's turn to pull on Natalie's sleeve. "Look! There's Nicole Morgan!"

"Oh I *love* her, she's got such a brilliant voice – did you hear her sing on 'Gold Dust' last year?"

"Yeah . . ." Natalie giggled. "But none of my friends from my old school are going to believe me when I tell them."

The girls were in a daze by the time they stopped in front of the ballroom. Emma smiled as she held open the door and ushered them in. "Fun, isn't it?" she whispered to Bella. Bella grinned and nodded. It wasn't just fun, it was a-maz-*ing*!

Bella stared as she walked into the

ballroom – last time she had been too nervous and excited to take everything in but now she was really determined to memorise every detail. The ballroom had been designed to look almost exactly like the Strictly Come Dancing studio. There was the huge dance floor, the banks of seats for the audience, and even the judges' panel at one side. And of course, hanging from the centre of the ceiling, the huge glitterball with its hundreds of tiny mirrors casting sparkling light all around the room. It was totally magical!

Bella spotted Jason coming in with the other Strictly Dance Academy boys from a door on the other side of the ballroom. Jason had been her partner in the

academy auditions and had been so nice
to her – even when she had seriously
embarrassed herself by falling over!
She caught his eye and waved and he
grinned and waved back.

Just then, Ben Goodwin strode in from
behind the boys and stood in the centre
of the room. Even though he was smiling
at them all, Bella felt her heart begin to
thump extra hard. What was the special
announcement going to be?

Ben clapped his hands together to get
everyone's attention. "Hello everybody!
And welcome to the Strictly Dance
Academy. We're really excited about
the group and hope you have a fabulous
time with us."

Bella exchanged a grin with Natalie

and Sofia – she knew they were thinking the same thing – they already *were* having a fabulous time!

"Usually, we'd start off with a tour of the school with your dorm monitors," Ben carried on. "But this time we're kicking everything off with something I think you'll find even more exciting . . ." He paused. "I'd like to introduce you to . . . the boy band New Ride!"

Everyone gasped. Bella heard excited whispers all around her but she was too stunned to speak. She *loved* New Ride! The four New Ride members walked through the door, smiling at everyone.

The drummer, Tyler, caught Bella's eye as he joined Ben Goodwin in the centre of the studio and winked. For a second

Bella felt dizzy – *Tyler from New Ride just winked at me!*

"Pretty cool, huh?" Sofia whispered in Bella's ear. Bella turned to her and saw that Sofia had turned pink with excitement!

"OK, let's get started," Ben called, holding his hands out to quiet everyone down. The murmurs died away. "Now, New Ride are performing this weekend at the London street carnival, which as you know is a world-famous event. They think that having some dancers on their float as they perform will help make it more of a spectacle." Ben grinned. "That's where *you* come in – they've decided to choose dancers from this academy so they're going to audition you to pick the four they need." Ben raised his eyebrows teasingly. "If you're interested, that is . . ."

Laughter and more excited murmurs broke out among the girls – dancing with New Ride? Who wouldn't be interested?

A girl at the back of the group called out. "When is the audition?"

Ben's grin got wider. "Right now."

Bella felt overwhelmed for a moment
– everything was happening so fast!
Even in her wildest dreams she'd never
imagined that she would have an
audition for a dancing role on her very
first day in the academy.

Ryan, the lead singer of New Ride,
stepped forward. "We just want to say
that we're sure that any of you girls
would be perfect for the gig, so try and

enjoy yourselves in the audition and
don't worry!"

"Easier said than done," whispered
Sofia.

Sofia was right – Bella's stomach was
already fizzing with nerves!

She began to warm up with the rest
of the girls. She would seriously love to
be one of the dancers for the New Ride
carnival gig but she knew it wasn't likely
she'd be picked – not when there were
so many more experienced dancers in
the group. Still, she'd just have to follow
her dad's advice again and remember
how she managed to get into the
academy in the first place – *dance like
nobody's watching.*

Miss Anna swept into the room with

Enrico, one of Strictly Come Dancing's
professional dancers. Bella
grinned. Enrico had taught
them the dance routine
they'd performed at the
auditions – if he was
teaching them again
maybe it would bring her
luck! Miss Anna clapped
her hands to get their
attention. "OK, listen
carefully everyone. Enrico
will pair you up with the
boys and then we will
learn a wonderful dance
for a carnival . . . Enrico's
speciality – the samba!"

Enrico quickly partnered

the girls and boys and Bella was
delighted to find herself with Jason
again.

"Don't be nervous," he told her. "I bet
you'll be great!"

"As long as I don't fall over again,"
Bella laughed. Suddenly she was
too excited to be nervous. More than
anything, she loved to dance – and that
was what she was about to do!

"The most important thing in the
samba is the bounce," Miss Anna told
them. "You must bend your knees while
you do the steps – this dance is all about
rhythm – and keeping it . . ."

Bella watched intently as Miss Anna
and Enrico showed them the dance. She
had done a little bit of samba in one of her

dance classes but this routine seemed
so much faster. All too soon it was time
to start trying it with their partners while
Miss Anna called out the steps.

"Back, together, back, together, back,
together, back – and don't forget to keep
the bounce on every step!"

At first Bella found it hard – especially
something called the volta step. But
once Enrico put on some carnival tracks,
she felt herself letting go and followed
the rhythm of the music. She suddenly
sensed her movements were coming
more naturally.

Enrico came and watched her dance
with Jason for a few moments. "That's
good, Bella," he said approvingly. "You
are *feeling* the music in your steps. Your

timing is excellent!"

When Enrico had moved on to look at one of the other couples, Jason gave her a gentle push on the shoulder. "See? I told you you'd be great!"

"I am having fun," Bella admitted. "But I don't know if it will be enough to get a gig with New Ride!"

A few minutes later, Ben Goodwin called them together for the audition. Bella felt her stomach cramp with nerves as the members of New Ride sat behind the judges' panel. Enrico sent them a good luck wink as Miss Anna signalled for the lights to go up on the floor. This was really it! Each couple had to perform separately, with Bella and Jason coming towards the end.

It's just like watching a Strictly Come Dancing show! Bella caught her breath as the spotlights followed the first couple as they moved across the dance floor.

Bella watched with crossed fingers as Natalie and Sofia danced great routines with their partners. She might not get into the carnival but it would be almost as good if her friends did! Then it was her turn. She suddenly felt shaky with nerves as she and Jason walked into the centre of the dance floor and took their positions. She wished that her dad was in the audience like he had been during the auditions. *That's it! I'll pretend he's there.* As the music started, Bella broke into a huge smile, imagining that her dad was out there cheering her on. She didn't think about the steps but just let her feet follow the rhythm of the music. Before she knew it, the routine was over and she could feel how huge her smile was – despite the nerves, she'd really enjoyed the dance!

"Well done," Jason whispered to her as they moved to make way for the next couple.

"You too," Bella whispered back.

After everyone had performed, Emma led the twenty dancers to another room down the hall to have a break while the decisions were being made. There were bottles of water and sandwiches but none of the girls were very hungry.

"It's hard to eat when you're waiting to find out if your dream's about to come true," Sofia said. Bella knew exactly what she meant.

Veronica didn't seem to be worried though. "I hope I'm paired with Ryan – he looked like he'd be able to dance quite well."

"You're pretty confident," Natalie said. "My mom always says it's best not to count your dancing shoes before they're made."

Veronica shrugged. "I think I've got reason to be – unlike *some* people."

Bella tried to ignore Veronica's look. She didn't know why Veronica seemed to dislike her so much but she was determined not to let it ruin the academy experience for her. It was hard though, when Veronica kept reminding her of the one thing Bella was worried about herself – her lack of experience.

After what seemed like hours but was probably only a few minutes, Emma called them back into the ballroom for the results. Sofia caught Bella's hand and squeezed it as they walked back up the corridor.

Here goes! thought Bella.

Ben Goodwin was standing with New

Ride. As soon
as they were
all gathered
back in the
ballroom,
he started to
speak. "Right,
girls. I won't
mess you about,
because I know
you'll all want
to be put out of
your misery. We
don't like keeping
people waiting for results – except for
a little bit on Strictly Come Dancing of
course!"

There was some nervous laughter.

"You all did really well and as Ryan said earlier, any of you would be great choices. But the four girls who we felt had something a bit special today and so will be dancing with New Ride at the carnival are: Natalie, Sofia, Veronica and Bella."

"Whoo-hooo!" Natalie cried out. She swivelled round to Bella and Sofia. "We did it!"

Bella felt her mouth drop open. She saw Jason give her a thumbs-up sign but it wasn't until Sofia grabbed her hands and started to whirl her round that she really believed it.

Her first day at the Strictly Dance Academy and she was going to be a dancer for New Ride!

As the rest of the Strictly pupils were taken off for their tour of the school, Bella, Natalie, Sofia and Veronica waited to hear what was going to happen next. *Wait until Dad hears about this!* Bella thought as she exchanged another round of grins with Natalie and Sofia.

The members of New Ride smiled and waved as they passed the girls on their

way out and Ben
Goodwin gave
them a wink
and said,
"Well danced,
girls!" before
disappearing
after them.

Miss Anna
clapped her hands to get their attention.
"Right, girls. I'll tell you who you'll be
dancing with in the band and then we
need to get you fitted for costumes – the
performance is this weekend so there's
no time to waste."

"This weekend? Wow!" Natalie
exclaimed.

Miss Anna smiled. "Yes, *wow!* But it

does mean we have to work very, very quickly. So, Bella, you will be dancing with the lead singer, Ryan. Natalie, you will be with Micky. Sofia, you will be with Tyler and Veronica, you will be with Tom. Now if you'll follow me I'll take you to meet the costume team and we can get going."

Miss Anna swept out of the door so quickly that the girls had to rush to keep up with her. As she hurried down the corridor, Bella kept thinking the same words over and over: *I'm dancing with the lead singer! I'm dancing with the lead singer!*

Moments later, Miss Anna was ushering them into a long room with clothes rails lining the walls on either

side. Bella
had never
seen so much
colour and
sparkle in
her life!

"It's like
Christmas
in clothes!"
she said.

"That's
exactly how we
like to think of it!" said Harriet as she
walked up to them. Bella remembered
her from the auditions. She'd been really
lovely, helping them all choose gorgeous
costumes. Today she was dressed in slim
black trousers with a wraparound red

wool top and her long black hair was twisted up into a French knot.

"If the Christmas lights on Oxford Street ever go down, we could definitely lend them our sparkles." A man laughed as he joined them. He was tall and dressed in jeans, a crisp white shirt and a suit jacket. Bella thought they both looked seriously smart. No wonder they were in costume design!

Miss Anna gestured towards the two costume designers. "Girls, you remember Harriet and Richard – they'll be making sure you get the right costumes for the carnival."

"And that you look after them properly!" Richard added with a frown.

He looked so stern for a moment that

Bella was worried but Harriet laughed.
"I'm sure they'll be careful," she told
him. She turned to the girls. "We have
to be strict, you see, because so much
work goes into these costumes. One tear
or stain can cause hundreds of pounds
worth of damage."

"We'll be really careful, we promise,"
Sofia said. She broke off as she caught
sight of a dress on the rails. "Oh! Look at
that green one!"

"This?" Richard pulled out a satin
emerald-green dress with two diamonds
cut out at the sides of the waist. The
neckline was covered in a swirling
pattern of silver and blue sequin flowers.

"It's gorgeous," Sofia sighed.

"Hmm," Harriet said. "Hold it up

against her for a sec."

Richard held it up in front of Sofia and tilted his head as he considered. "Interesting . . ."

"Yes," Harriet nodded. "You're lucky, it's hard to wear green. It doesn't suit every complexion. But with your olive skin . . ."

"And your dark hair," Richard added, "you can definitely pull it off."

"Best try it on so we can see what adjustments we'll need to make," Harriet told Sofia. "It's a samba cut so it'll fall just right for the dance, but we may have to take it in a bit."

A delighted Sofia took the dress into the changing cubicle at the back of the room.

"Now, let's see what we can find for the rest of you," Harriet said.

"I want *this* one," Veronica said, marching up to the clothes rail. She pulled out a dress in a gold satin with layered ruffles around the collar and the skirt. Gold sequins in tiny star and moon shapes lined the neckline and the sides.

Bella looked longingly at it – it was exactly the kind of dress she would have loved to wear. *But it doesn't matter, they're all gorgeous*, she thought.

"This is perfect for me," Veronica said, swirling the dress around in front of her.

"Careful!" Miss Anna said. "Don't forget what you've been told about taking care of the dresses. And it's the costume designers who will be deciding what you will wear – they're really experienced in dressing dancers for shows."

"And I'm afraid the costume designers don't think this is the right one for you," Harriet said gently.

Richard nodded. "It's too warm a

tone for your skin, you need something cooler."

"But I wear gold all the time!" Veronica protested, her lower lip jutting out.

"Not this gold," Harriet said firmly. She took it from Veronica and was about to hang it up when she stopped and looked at Bella. "Wait a moment . . ."

"Oh yes," Richard said. "It's definitely right for her."

Harriet held up the dress against Bella and nodded. "There. That's you sorted out. Why don't you go and try it on?"

Bella couldn't believe it! She was getting to wear the very dress she would have chosen! As she turned, she caught Veronica's eye and tried to make an

apologetic face – she did feel bad that
Veronica wasn't getting to wear the
dress she wanted. But Veronica just

scowled at her and
turned her back.

"Ignore her, she's
just got a dose of
the divas," Natalie
whispered to her.

Bella went off to
try on the dress,
deciding not to let
Veronica upset her.
"And now for you
two!" Harriet was
saying.

A few minutes
later, the four girls

were standing in front of the floor-to-ceiling mirror at the very back of the room. Harriet and Richard had found a bright pink dress striped with sequins in a deeper pink for Natalie and an ice-blue and silver dress for Veronica. Bella thought the blue dress really suited Veronica, highlighting her mass of curly blonde hair, but Veronica's grumpy glance at Bella told her she was still annoyed not to be wearing the gold. All the dresses were in what Harriet and Richard called a samba cut so the girls did look part of a group even though they were in different colours.

"There's only one word for the way you look," Harriet told them.

"What's that?" asked Natalie.

"Fab-u-*lous!*" Harriet and Richard said together.

That's just how I feel, too! thought Bella.

5

Bella's first week at the academy whizzed by. Between the dance classes, school lessons and the samba rehearsals for the New Ride carnival performance, Bella had never worked so hard in her life! She felt absolutely exhausted.

When she warmed up before each dance lesson, muscles she never knew she had began to ache! But she was determined not to fall behind any of the

other more experienced dancers and so
she squeezed as much extra practice
as she could manage into her busy
schedule.

On Friday morning, Bella found an
empty dance studio in the academy
to practise her routine. She'd been
getting more nervous every day. It was
one thing dancing for an audition in a
closed room, it was something else when
you were going to be dancing with the
lead singer from New Ride in front of
thousands of people! Every time she
thought about it, she felt as if her insides
were doing the samba too . . .

"Back, together, back, together, back,
together, back," she chanted as she
went through the steps one more time.

She knew she had the bounce of the dance now but she wanted to be sure that every single move was just perfect. There was no way she wanted to let anyone down!

"Good to see you working hard," said a voice from the door.

Bella spun around to see Pam, the cleaning lady. Bella had met her just before her

audition when she and Sofia had seen
Pam doing a tango with her broom! She
was holding a bucket and mop and her
wrinkled face was creased into a wide
smile.

"Oh hello!" Bella said, feeling a little
embarrassed. "I was just practising a
dance I'm supposed to do—"

"With a certain famous boy band, I've
heard," Pam chuckled. "I wouldn't mind
dancing with that Ryan myself." Pam
wiggled her hips.

Bella laughed. "Am I in your way?"

Pam shook her head. "Don't you worry
– the floor can wait. The important thing
is for you to remember the bounce in
the samba. Keep practising until it's
completely natural to you." She bent her

knees and did a couple of samba steps with her mop.

"I'll do my best," Bella said.

"I'm sure you will," Pam smiled. "The secret is to keeeep dancing!" She turned and samba-stepped out the door, her bucket clanking as she went.

Bella decided to do the routine one more time. As Pam had said, she just had to keep dancing . . .

When she was finished, she put her hands on her hips and stared in the mirror. *Well, Bella Jones, if you don't know it now you never will*, she thought to herself.

A moment later, Natalie burst through the dance studio door, making Bella jump with surprise.

"*There* you are! I've been looking for you everywhere!"

"What's the matter?" Bella was suddenly panicky – maybe the gig had been cancelled! She was really nervous but that didn't mean she didn't want to do it!

"You have to come NOW or you'll be late for English class – and you know what Mr Dival is like!"

The two girls dashed out of the rehearsal studio and rushed down the hall. They took the stairs to the second floor two at a time and arrived at the classroom panting. Bella pushed through the door into the academy classroom with Natalie just behind her.

"Thank goodness! He's not here yet," Bella said breathlessly to Natalie. "Thanks for coming to get me – being told off is not my idea of a fun way to start the day!" She collapsed into her seat, breathing hard.

"No problem," Natalie slid into her seat. "But next time you decide to make a break for it, choose somewhere a little closer to the classroom, OK?"

Bella laughed. "OK!"

Veronica shot a smug look over at them. "If you're that unfit, I don't know

how you're going to manage the samba
with New Ride . . ."

Natalie rolled her eyes. "We'll make it
somehow, thanks, Veronica."

Mark, one of the boys in the academy,
leaned back in his seat towards Bella.
"So how's it going to work with New
Ride? Are you doing just one dance?"

Bella smiled. "We're doing a couple
of set pieces with our partners in the
band—"

"It's *three* set pieces, not a couple,"
Veronica interrupted.

"And we'll be doing a group routine,"
Bella continued, trying to ignore the
interruption.

"Actually, we're doing the group
routine *first*," Veronica said.

Bella felt her cheeks grow hot. Mark must think she was really stupid with Veronica correcting her every word!

"And do the set pieces last for the whole song?" Mark asked.

Bella was about to answer when Veronica broke in again. "No, they start in the middle of the songs. The singers sing the intros without any dancing."

"He was asking *Bella* you know," Natalie said, frowning at Veronica.

Mark coughed and turned round in his seat. Suddenly the atmosphere felt really awkward and Bella wished the teacher would arrive to put an end to it all.

"There's no point in asking amateurs for their opinion," Veronica said. "They never get it right. And Bella's already proved she's not experienced enough for this show – if she's so exhausted after just a couple of days of rehearsal how is she going to cope with the real thing?"

"She's not going to *cope*, she's going to be brilliant!" said Natalie sharply.

"Well if she can't it isn't a problem," Veronica's voice had a fake-sweet tone. "Because she can just give up dancing with the lead singer and her place *and* her costume to someone who *can* cope with it." She smiled at them all and it was clear that what she meant was *she* could take over.

Natalie took a breath to say more but at that moment the door swung open and Mr Dival came in, slapping down a pile of papers on his desk.

There was only time to flash Natalie
a weak grateful smile before Bella
had to face the front and pretend to be
paying attention to what Mr Dival was
saying about their next spelling test.
She shivered, feeling like she'd been
dunked into a bucket of ice. What if
Veronica was right? It was true that she
was exhausted after just a few
days of rehearsing. Was
that because she was so
inexperienced?

*Maybe I'm going to
ruin everything!* Bella
thought.

I ♡ New Ride

Suddenly all her excitement dissolved away, leaving her jittery with worry. The last thing she wanted was to let her friends and family down – let alone all the band members of New Ride. *Veronica's probably right*, Bella thought miserably. *She's the one who should be dancing with Ryan and wearing the gold dress . . .*

6

The next morning, Bella thought there was no way she could dance. Her legs felt like cotton wool and when she picked up her dress, she saw that her hands were shaking. She stroked the satin of the skirt and closed her eyes, trying to think positive, confident thoughts, but Veronica's words from yesterday kept creeping in.

"How are you going to bear to let it go?"

Bella opened her eyes to see Sofia smiling at her. Sofia pointed at the dress. "You know you have to give the dress back afterwards, right?" she teased.

Bella nodded, trying to smile, but Sofia narrowed her eyes as she examined Bella's face. "Hey, you're really worried, aren't you?"

"A bit," Bella said. *A lot*, she thought.

"You're going to be great," Sofia told her. "Remember, you were picked to dance with the lead singer!"

"Probably by mistake," Veronica said, as she passed by.

"It was no mistake," Natalie said, glaring at her. "You're just jealous."

Veronica looked back over her shoulder and laughed. "Jealous? Of *Bella*? I don't think so!"

"Just ignore her," Natalie told Bella after Veronica had left. "She *is* jealous you know."

"Thanks, you two," Bella said, feeling cheered up by her friends' support. "You're the best!"

*

Half an hour later, Miss Anna and the four girls were standing in the large car park where the carnival was going to set off from. She led them through the throngs of people to a temporary caravan that had been designated as New Ride's dressing room.

"The band are still setting up for the dress rehearsal," Miss Anna told them. "Harriet and Richard said you should hang up your dresses on this rack by the door."

"I'm not leaving my dress there! What if someone comes in and steals it?"

"I don't think that's likely, Veronica," Miss Anna said calmly. "It's very safe here."

"Well, I don't want my dress next to theirs anyway. Their sequins could catch on mine and make a hole or something." Veronica held up her dress in the air as if it might be damaged just by being

close to the others.

Miss Anna sighed.

"Very well, then, Veronica.

You can put your dress wherever you think best."

Veronica flounced off and found another hanging space in a corner, tucked behind some of New Ride's equipment.

Natalie rolled her eyes as she hung her pink dress where Miss Anna had told her to. "Guess who's got another dose of the divas?" she whispered.

Sofia and Bella giggled as they put their dresses next to Natalie's. "Ve*rrr*y ridiculous, as my mother would say!" Sofia said.

"Now," Miss Anna said. "There is still an hour before the dress rehearsal, so if you'd like to take a look at the other acts, you can go out to the staging area outside. That's where the carnival will set off from when it starts."

"I'm too hungry," Sofia said. "If I don't go and have something to eat I might faint during the rehearsal!"

Miss Anna laughed. "That certainly

wouldn't make a good start to the
carnival," she said. "You'd better run to
the canteen at the back of the car park
and get yourself a snack."

"Well I'm not bothered about going
to watch a bunch of random people,"
Veronica said. "I'm going to go
and warm up properly – that's what
professionals do," she added, shooting a
look at Bella.

"Well, *I'm* going to go and look,"
Natalie said. "I've never been to the
carnival before and I don't want to miss
a thing! Come on, Bella, you'll come
with me won't you?"

Bella felt torn. She wanted to go and
see the acts, but maybe she should
spend the time warming up and

happen when they found out the dresses had completely disappeared!

Sofia entered at that moment with Veronica following just behind. "What's wrong with you two?" she asked.

"Probably realised they're not up to dancing with New Ride," Veronica said, walking to the corner of the caravan where she'd hung her dress.

"Our costumes are gone!" Bella said.

"*What?*" Sofia stared, her eyes wide with shock. "But how? *Where* have they gone?"

"We don't know," Natalie said. "But we'd better find out quick, because the rehearsal starts in less than half an hour!"

"Well, *my* dress is still here," Veronica

said smugly, emerging from her corner carrying her blue dress. "I did tell you that leaving them there wasn't a good idea."

"Yeah, *thanks*, Veronica," snapped Natalie. "That doesn't help us figure out what we're going to do, does it?"

Veronica shrugged.

She doesn't seem surprised that our dresses have gone missing, Bella thought. *That's odd*.

"I shouldn't worry too much," Veronica said airily. "If your dresses don't turn up, I can do the dances solo."

Bella, Natalie and Sofia looked at each other – they didn't like that idea *at all*!

7

Veronica smiled. "Excuse me, I think I'd better get dressed – I don't want to be late for the dress rehearsal." She walked towards the curtained off area. "And like I said, don't worry, if you don't find your dresses, I'll be happy to step in for you."

"Not likely!" Natalie burst out.

"But if we can't find our costumes, what *are* we going to do?" Bella said.

"Miss Anna isn't here to ask."

"Let's go look for them," Sofia said. "Maybe someone moved them without realising what they were for."

"Good idea!" Bella felt her hopes rising. Maybe it was just a simple mistake . . . But did they have enough time to solve the problem before the rehearsal began?

*

Outside, Bella's spirits sank. There were dozens of people rushing to and fro. The floats had arrived and there were the sounds of hammering as last-minute decorations were nailed into place. How would they find their costumes with so much going on?

"Come on, let's ask someone," Natalie

said, hurrying forward into the crowd.
She went up to a man in a rainbow-
striped suit wearing a red curly wig.
"Excuse, me, have you seen anyone
carrying a pile of costumes? Gold, pink
and green?"

The man stopped and scratched his
head, making the wig tilt on to his
forehead. "Costumes? Hmm. I did see a
girl with blonde hair carrying
a stack of dresses a few
minutes ago. She
went that way." He
pointed the way and
then readjusted his
wig. "You girls in the
carnival?"

"We are if we can find

those costumes," Sofia told him.

"Well, good luck to you then. Hope you find them!"

So do we! Bella thought as she hurried after the others. She couldn't help wondering who the girl with the blonde hair had been but there was no time to waste thinking about it – they had to get hold of those dresses!

They rushed through the small crowd that was building up until Natalie suddenly stopped dead ahead of them.

"What is it?" Bella craned round Natalie to see what she was looking at.

"It's a dumpster!" Natalie looked at Bella and Sofia, her eyes wide with horror. "I think Veronica's tried to stop us being in the show by getting rid of the dresses!"

"You think Veronica threw them away?" Bella felt herself go cold. Even though she'd been feeling suspicious herself, until now she hadn't thought it was really possible that Veronica would do anything *that* horrible.

"I don't think she could have done it," Sofia said. "After I went to get something to eat I was sitting near Veronica while she did her warm-up – she was in my sight nearly the whole time."

"*Nearly* the whole time," Natalie said. "It is still possible though."

"I suppose so," Sofia said, frowning. "If she'd been really quick."

"Well there's only one way to find out," said Bella. She took a deep breath and went up close to the dumpster. It was too tall to see into but there were some orange plastic crates on the ground. She pulled them over and stacked them into a make-shift set of steps. Natalie and Sofia helped hold them steady as she climbed up to peer inside.

"Can you see anything?" Natalie called to her.

Bella blinked and squinted to see the contents of the dark dumpster. She saw bottles, cans, planks of splintered wood and . . . yes, there on top was a pile of cloth. Bella's heart jumped as she leaned over the edge of the dumpster to get a better look. Then her shoulders relaxed. It wasn't a pile of dresses – what she was looking at was a large pile of trimmings and scraps of rough cloth – the kind she'd just seen on the floats for the carnival. There was absolutely nothing in there that looked like their missing costumes.

Bella scrambled back down the crates. "They're not there," she told them.

Sofia looked relieved. "Well at least we know that Veronica hasn't done anything with them."

Natalie nodded. "Yeah, that's good. But it doesn't get us any closer to finding out where the dresses *have* gone. We've been following the wrong trail!"

"And now it's definitely time for the dress rehearsal," Bella said. "What are we going to do?"

"There's only one thing we can do," Sofia said. "We'll have to rehearse in our ordinary clothes and hope we can figure something out in time for the carnival."

"What will New Ride think?" Natalie cried.

"We don't have time to worry about that," said Bella. "We have to get to the rehearsal!"

They arrived at the staging area with only seconds to spare. New Ride were already in place and gave the three girls a friendly wave.

"They don't seem to care that we're not in costume," Bella whispered to Natalie.

"Let's hope it stays that way!" Natalie said.

Veronica came over from where she'd

been practising some steps. She looked
them up and down. "Oh dear, no luck
finding your costumes then? What a
pity . . ." She laughed.

Natalie glared at her. "Yeah, OK,
Veronica, we know you're really pleased
about it."

Miss Anna rushed up. "Why aren't you
in costume, girls?"

Bella took a breath to answer her but
Miss Anna shook her head. "No, never
mind, there's no time now. You'll just
have to rehearse as you are and then get
changed afterwards. Quickly now, go
and take your places!"

Bella rushed across the room with
Natalie and Sofia. As she took her first
position, she felt her stomach turn over.

What would Miss Anna say when she found out there were no costumes to get changed into? As the band began to play she forced herself to focus. She might feel silly dancing in her ordinary clothes with Veronica next to her in a proper samba dress, but she knew she had to do the best she could. She had to prove she deserved the chance she'd been given. *Professionals shouldn't mind what they're wearing*, she thought as New Ride started to play.

As Bella took her first steps, she found herself dancing without thinking. She had practised so hard that her body knew just what to do. She began to enjoy herself so much that she forgot to be nervous. When it came to the first of

her dances with Ryan her heart started
racing. She was really dancing with the
lead singer of New Ride! Ryan might be
a singer but he was clearly used to
learning dance routines.

It felt as if
they were
gliding
from one
move to the next. Their
volta steps went perfectly!
Bella felt herself break into
an enormous smile. This was
seriously cool!

The set routines with Ryan
went without a single hitch and
the group routine with Natalie,
Sofia and Veronica was so

much fun that Bella forgot they weren't actually at the carnival yet! They had just begun the last of the routines when Bella heard someone shouting.

"No, no, NO!"

The band stopped with a clatter of drums and a screeching sound from one of the microphones. Bella stumbled, startled at the sudden stop to the music. She looked round to see New Ride's manager standing glaring at them.

"Why are these girls not in

costume? The carnival is due to begin in a few minutes and here they are in jeans and T-shirts!"

Miss Anna stepped forward. "I think they just ran out of time, Mr Burns."

"Well they need to be in the right costumes. We can't have New Ride appearing with dancers looking like *that*." Mr Burns said, pointing at Bella.

Bella felt her cheeks burn. She knew that he was only talking about what she was wearing but it was hard not to think he might mean her dancing too. She glanced over at Natalie and Sofia, who made gestures as if to say, *What are we going to do?*

"It's not a problem," Miss Anna said calmly. "The girls can get changed now."

It was time to own up. "Actually, Miss Anna," Bella began, "we can't."

Miss Anna lifted her eyebrows in surprise. "What? Why ever not, Bella?"

"Because our costumes have disappeared!" Natalie burst out. "We went back to the dressing room and they'd gone!"

"Then why is that girl wearing her dress then?" Mr Burns snapped, waving his hand at Veronica.

"Because I left my dress in a safe place," Veronica said smugly. "I did *try* and tell the girls not to leave their costumes on the rack by the door, but they didn't listen."

"Yes, all right, Veronica," said Miss Anna, shooting her a disapproving glance. She turned to Mr Burns. "I'm sure we can sort this out," she told him.

"As far as I'm concerned, it *is* sorted," he said. "The girl who's got her costume on will dance, and the others won't. And that's the end of it."

"But Mr Burns!" Miss Anna exclaimed.

"I'm sorry," said Mr Burns in a grumpy voice. Bella thought he didn't sound sorry at all! "But the carnival is going to start any minute and we haven't got time to waste trying to find lost dresses."

Bella felt her insides contract with disappointment. She had been really enjoying the rehearsal and had finally overcome her worry about being good enough to perform with New Ride – and now she wasn't going to dance after all!

Ryan stepped forward and touched her arm. "I'm really sorry you won't be dancing – I thought you were great," he said.

Bella's eyes welled up with tears as she tried to smile at him. She couldn't believe it – she'd been about to do her first ever public performance and now it had been taken away from her! She knew it wasn't Mr Burns' fault – he was trying to do the right thing for the band – but she wished he'd been a bit less grumpy about it. She exchanged glances with Natalie and Sofia, who both looked equally upset. She tried to ignore the triumphant smile Veronica was wearing as she walked away from the band.

Something Bella's dad had said to her a long time ago popped into her head. *Sometimes you have to pretend to be brave and then you become brave.* Bella lifted her head. *She* was going to pretend to be brave. At least then she might be able to make Natalie and Sofia feel better. She grabbed their hands as they came to stand beside her. She might not have the carnival to look forward to, but at least she had two great friends!

Miss Anna had come up to them. "I'm so sorry, girls," she began. But she was interrupted by the sound of Harriet and Richard running through the door.

"Hang on!" Harriet called. "You can't dance without these!"

Bella felt her mouth drop open in shock.

"You found the dresses!" Natalie cried out, jumping into the air with excitement.

"What do you mean?" Richard smiled, as he held out Natalie's pink dress with Sofia's green one. "They were never lost."

"We decided they would look even better if we customised them," Harriet explained, holding out Bella's dress.  On all three dresses, the girls' names had been embroidered in gold and silver sequins.

"My name in sequins!" Natalie shouted. "Wow!"

Sofia grinned. "They look beautiful, thank you!"

"Thank you!" Bella said, still too shocked to understand what had happened.

"What's going on?" Veronica demanded, striding up to them.

"I'm sorry, Veronica, but we couldn't find your dress when we went to fetch them,"

Richard said. "It wasn't where we'd told Miss Anna to get you to leave them so yours will have to stay as it is."

Veronica's face dropped for a second and then she perked up. "But it's too late for them to be in the carnival anyway. Mr Burns said so."

Miss Anna turned to Mr Burns, who had walked up to see what was going on. "The rest of the costumes are here now, Mr Burns. Can the girls dance in the carnival if they get dressed straightaway?"

Mr Burns checked his watch. "As long as they're in costume and ready to go in five minutes, I don't see why not."

Miss Anna turned to Bella, Natalie and Sofia. "You heard him – off you go!"

Bella, Natalie and Sofia didn't need telling twice. They raced to the dressing room and got into their dresses in seconds, thrust their feet into their shoes and ran back to the band.

Mr Burns met them at the door. He looked them up and down and then

smiled for the first time. "Those dresses
are first rate, they'll make a great
impression on the float." He turned to
Veronica. "Shame you didn't leave your
dress where you were supposed to – the
designers have done a grand job."

Veronica's face turned bright pink
and her eyebrows knitted together into
a deep frown. As the girls got on to the
float outside with the members of New
Ride, Miss Anna had to remind Veronica
to smile.

There was no need for Bella to be
reminded to smile – she broke into a grin
every time she looked down at her dress
with her name glittering in sequins. *This
must be what it feels like to be on Strictly
Come Dancing!* she thought. She hoped

her dad had a good position in the
crowds that were lining the street – she
knew he'd be proud of her for getting
into the carnival. She was certainly
proud to be here!

Just before New Ride began to play,
Ryan leaned forward and whispered in
Bella's ear. "It's great
you made it in the
end!"

As Bella started
to dance she
thought
how right
that was
– she *had*
made it in
the end!

The float
rolled down
the street
and as the
people
watching
caught sight
of the names
sparkling
on the girls'
dresses,
they
began to
cheer. "Go
Bella! Go Natalie!
Go Sofia!"

The three girls
exchanged grins as
they began their next
routine. What an
incredible carnival
– it was the best
day ever!

*And it's even
better because
I'm sharing
it with my
friends*, Bella
thought,
sending
another smile
into the crowd.

See how Bella and her friends
learn to Rock 'n' Roll in

Read on for a sneak peek ...

Humming to herself, Bella Jones
finished brushing her hair and put on
her lucky sparkly earrings. She usually
only wore these on special occasions,
but she had a feeling that today might
just turn out to be one of them.

Mind you, she thought, smiling at
her reflection and smoothing down a
stray strand of hair, ever since she'd
auditioned and earned herself a place

at the Strictly Dance Academy, *every* day had become special. Bella still couldn't quite believe that she was now living and training at the famous London dance school, and was loving every minute. Talk about a dream come true!

"Aaargh!" came a cross voice just then. Bella turned in surprise, only to see a tap shoe whizzing through the air. Natalie, one of her roommates, was peering into her wardrobe, throwing out clothes, shoes and everything else as she searched for something. "Where *are* they?" she wailed.

"What are you looking for?" Bella asked. She had met Natalie at their first audition for the academy and liked her immediately. Natalie was American, and a real livewire – fun, bouncy and energetic. She didn't seem very happy today though.

"I can't find my favourite ballet shoes," she grumbled, running a hand through her tight dark curls. "You haven't seen them, have you? I've hunted everywhere!"

"No," Bella replied, "but I'll help you look."

"Me too," offered Sofia, who also

shared the room. She was half-Italian and had gorgeous long black hair and olive skin. As well as being kind and loyal, she was also a brilliant dancer, and the three girls had really hit it off since joining the academy. Recently, they'd all been lucky enough to get picked to dance with the famous boy band New Ride at a carnival too. Now *that* was something none of them would forget in a hurry!

With a graceful leap from her bed, Sofia joined Bella and Natalie by the wardrobe which was rapidly becoming empty. "They've got to be here *somewhere*," Natalie said, tossing a pink leotard over her shoulder.

"Looking for these, by any chance?" a

smug voice called out.

Bella, Natalie and Sofia swung round to see Veronica, the fourth member of their dorm in the doorway. She walked in, gingerly holding a pair of ballet shoes by the tips of her fingers as if worried she might catch something from them.

Natalie leapt to her feet. "My shoes! Thanks, dude! Where did you find them?"

Veronica looked horrified to be called "dude". She was blonde, pretty and a major snob. "I must have picked them up by mistake," she replied coolly. "They're far too big for me, of course. What gigantic feet you have, Natalie!"

Bella winced, wishing Veronica wouldn't be so mean. She wasn't convinced Veronica had picked up the shoes by mistake either. It would be just like her to take them on purpose, knowing it would send Natalie into a panic.

Natalie wasn't the sort of person you could push around though. She snatched her shoes and glared back defiantly. "So what does that make you, Princess Dainty-toes?" she scoffed. She pointed at her name which had been written inside each shoe. "See? Next time CHECK!"

Uh-oh. Now Veronica looked positively murderous. "Guys," Bella said quickly, trying to smooth things over. "Let's just calm down a bit ..."

But Veronica was in no mood to calm down. "Don't you *dare* speak to me like that!" she hissed at Natalie, her eyes blazing. "Or I'll—"

**Read
Rock 'n' Rolling
to find out what
happens next!**

Meet the characters at *Strictly Dance Academy*

Character profile:

Sofia

★ Age: 9

★ Favourite colour: red

★ Favourite dance: the samba – because it's the party dance!

★ Favourite outfit: Sofia loves the short white dress with red polka dots that she wears in *Rock 'n' Rolling*.

★ Favourite accessory: her red and silver hair band that sparkles against her dark hair.

★ Favourite dance partner: definitely Tyler, the drummer from New Ride!

★ Sofia started dancing as soon as she could walk – trying to copy her mother's beautiful ballet moves!

Fun fact *Sofia's mother was a famous prima ballerina in Italy and has been taking Sofia to watch the ballet since she was only three years old!*

WIN TICKETS!

THE LIVE TOUR

THE STARS FROM STRICTLY COME DANCING ARE COMING TO A VENUE NEAR YOU!

Straight from the hit BBC1 TV show, the celebrity dancers and their partners will perform their spectacular dance routines on tour in front of the judges. And you have the chance to watch the live show and vote for your favourite act!

Read our Strictly Come Dancing books *Tango Tangle* and *Samba Sensation*, answer the questions below and soon you and your family could be off to see the exciting live tour of Strictly Come Dancing!

QUESTION 1
What does Bella's dad tell her to do in *Tango Tangle*?

a) Dance like nobody's watching
b) Dance with a happy heart
c) Dance with a spring in your step

QUESTION 2
What is the name of the boy band
in *Samba Sensation*?

a) New Ride
b) New Look
c) New Direction

**JUST SEND YOUR ANSWERS, WITH YOUR NAME
AND ADDRESS, ON A POSTCARD TO:**
Strictly Come Dancing Competition, Marketing Department,
Hodder Children's Books, 338 Euston Road, London, NW1 3BH.

BY 30 NOVEMBER 2012.

Or enter at WWW.HODDERCHILDRENS.CO.UK

THE PRIZE
A family ticket for 4 to see Strictly Come Dancing The Live Tour at one
of the participating venues in January or February 2013.

The prize is for the tickets only. Winners must make their own way to the venue.
No cash alternative offered. Travel, accommodation and associated costs
are not included. Tickets are not transferable.

See full terms and conditions at www.hodderchildrens.co.uk

And 50 runner-up prizes are also available!

Join our Review Crew and receive a free book!*

Be the first to read great new books!

The Review Crew are a group of passionate readers who help us by reviewing new and upcoming books before they've even hit the shops!

Members of the Review Crew receive free copies of our books in manuscript form and tell us what they think by filling in a simple questionnaire. We also like to ask for feedback about cover designs.

If you'd like to claim your free book and join the hundreds of other kids getting involved, just visit:

www.hachettechildrens.co.uk/reviewcrew

and sign up today!

Or, fill in the form overleaf and post to: Review Crew, Hachette Children's Books, 338 Euston Road, London, NW1 3BH

Join our Review Crew
and receive a free book!*

Be the first to read great new books!

The Review Crew are a group of passionate readers
who help us by reviewing new and upcoming books
before they've even hit the shops!

Members of the Review Crew receive free copies of our
books in manuscript form and tell us what they think by
filling in a simple questionnaire. We also like to ask
for feedback about cover designs.

**If you'd like to claim your free book and join the
hundreds of other kids getting involved, just visit:**

www.hachettechildrens.co.uk/reviewcrew

and sign up today!

Or, fill in the form overleaf and post to: Review Crew, Hachette
Children's Books, 338 Euston Road, London, NW1 3BH

*All free books worth a minimum £3.99. Please allow 28 days for delivery. UK only.